THE ADVENTURES OF SPARKY

By
Norman J Vaughan-Cubitt

AuthorHouse™ UK Ltd.
1663 Liberty Drive
Bloomington, IN 47403 USA
www.authorhouse.co.uk
Phone: 0800.197.4150

Published by AuthorHouse 10/22/2013

ISBN: 978-1-4918-8208-5 (sc)
ISBN: 978-1-4918-8209-2 (e)

About The Author

He was born in Exeter in Devon England in 1946.

His father died when he was three, and, because his mother became ill shortly thereafter, he was placed in a children's home until he was 10.

Having failed his 11 plus exam, he left school at the age of 15 and worked at many different jobs until he enlisted into the army at the age of 17.

He spent most of his 9 army years in Germany and after leaving the forces he remained in Germany to work for NAAFI.

In 1979, he married an English woman, Thelma, who he met in Germany and to whom he is with now.

They returned to England in 1994 and purchased a small cottage near Canterbury, Kent bringing with them 6 cats and 1 dog.

He now works in retail selling furniture for the aptly named "Knot Just Furniture" which is a family owned Company.

He and Thelma have had many pets during their time together and it was this that led him to write The Adventures of Sparky.

About The Book.

This is the story of a little dog called Sparky who unfortunately gets lost.

It tells of the Adventures he has as he tries to find his way back home.

He makes lots of friends and enemies too and also manages to find time

for a little romance.

Read how he finds a best friend in Nelson, a one eyed cat and how he

meets and makes friends with the Cat gang.

He meets a lot of other animals on the way but beware of Brutus the very

big dog and then of course there is the deadly Rat Pack.

Sit back, relax and enjoy The Adventures of Sparky.

Sparky and Phoebe are the only pets mentioned in this book, that are still

alive and they plus the cats names and the three Kimmies are pets that

Thelma and I have owned since we have been together.

By ...N. J. Vaughan - Cubitt.

Chapter One ..... Sparky.

Sparky was a small dog with a pointed nose and pointed ears. He had big brown eyes which seemed to be smiling. His legs were short but he could still run quite fast. His tail was bent, rather like a question mark.

This was a birth fault but Sparky, not knowing it was a birth fault, did in fact, quite like it. He could lay it down along his back and the fur would stand up like the hair of a hedgehog when it is angry.

His fur was dark with light streaks here and there and felt rather hard, not the soft type of fur that a lot of dogs have. He had white softer fur running from under his chin and all the way down past his chest to his tummy.

For fun he enjoyed chasing the birds, butterflies and other flying insects that came into his garden. He lived in a small cottage in the country with his owner, who was called Granny Thelma.

She was quite an elderly lady with grey hair. She was quite tubby and always wore an apron. She wore glasses which sometimes slid to the end of her nose and she would often sing to herself as she went around the house cleaning and tidying.

This gave Sparky great comfort for he always knew where she was.

Sometimes they would pass the time playing ball in the garden, which she would throw and he would chase and return to her so that she could throw it again.

A wide track ran along the back fence. At times small children would pass along the gate at the back of the garden and call to Granny Thelma and she would give them apples from the big tree which stood in the centre of the garden and they would lean over the fence and stroke Sparky and he enjoyed these times.

Sometimes, he and Granny Thelma would go for walks in the woods beyond the garden but they never went further than that because after the woods, was a large hill which Granny Thelma could not climb.

In the evenings, Granny Thelma would feed him and make some food for herself and sometimes, if she had any left over on her plate, she would give it to him as a treat.

When they had eaten, she would settle down into her large armchair with her feet resting on a footstool. Sparky would jump up onto her lap or onto the small settee near to her chair, cuddle in and go to sleep.

This was Sparky's favourite room, for it was in here that he spent most of his time when he was not in the garden or out walking.

The cottage in which they lived was quite small. It had Granny Thelma's bedroom upstairs and another room into which she seldom went. This was in fact a spare bedroom but because she and Sparky lived alone, the room was not used.

Downstairs there was the kitchen, the bathroom and the living room. Granny Thelma often wished that the bathroom was upstairs so that, if she needed the bathroom at night, she would not have to go downstairs and then need to clime back up the stairs again which she sometimes found quite difficult.

There was a door, that lead out into the front of the house, but Granny Thelma would never let Sparky out through that door, he always went out through the back door and into the garden. .

There were times during the day when Granny Thelma would go out alone leaving him to play by himself. When she returned she would be carrying some bags containing food and other items and sometimes she would give him a new toy such as a ball or a squeaky shaped bone.

He had quite a few toys and at times when Granny Thelma did not want to play because she was tired or busy, he would take a toy and play alone with it.

In the living room next to the armchair there stood an old broken settee which had a torn cloth covering and broken springs.

Sparky loved this settee for it was here that he hid his toys and sometimes he slept on it. Dogs love to hide things even their food and this was Sparky's special hiding place and it was because he hid his toys in the settee that he would find himself on a great adventure.

Chapter Two ……..Sparky Gets Lost.

Other than the times that Granny Thelma had taken Sparky for walks he

had never been outside and other than the birds, butterflies and other

flying insects that flew in the garden, he had never seen any other animal

and meeting other animals would add to the adventure that he would soon

find himself caught up in.

On the morning of the day that Sparky's adventure was to begin, he was

in the garden playing with one of his toys when he heard a loud noise

coming from the other side of the garden fence.

He thought that the noise was from the wagon that came to collect the

rubbish but it was not, it was very loud and having never seen it before,

he ran and hid behind the apple tree that stood in the centre of the lawn.

The noise stopped and suddenly a man who he had never seen before and

who was very big,opened the gate and walked up to the back door.

He banged with his fist rather loudly upon the door. This frightened

Sparky even more and he tried to make himself seem smaller, hoping that the man would not see him.

After a few moments the door opened and Granny Thelma welcomed the man with a smile. This relaxed Sparky a little but he remained hidden.

As the man went into the house the gate opened and another man came into the garden and went into the house as well.

After a little while the door opened and the 2 men came out carrying the broken settee in which all of Sparky's toys were hidden. They carried the broken settee into the back of the lorry and dropped it roughly onto the floor. Having done that they picked up a new settee and carried it into the house.

"O dear" said Sparky to himself, "they are taking my settee and all of my toys away, I must rescue them" and, seeing that the gate was opened, he ran across the garden, through the gate and jumped into the back of the lorry which he thought was a dark room.

He sprang onto the old settee and began searching for his toys. They were well hidden but as he found one, he threw it to one side but because he was busy he did not note the passing of time.

Suddenly he heard the men returning to the lorry which scared him so he jumped from the settee and found a place behind it to hide.

He could see through a gap in the settee and saw the men close the doors of the lorry with a loud slam which frightened Sparky even more, so he stayed still and quiet, wondering what was happening and not realising that he was being locked in.

After a few moments he heard another loud noise which was the sound of the engine being started and with a sudden lurch the lorry began to move. He tried to bark but was so afraid that when he opened his mouth nothing seemed to come out and not knowing what was happening or even if he would ever get out into the open again Sparky started to cry.

He had never been so afraid and all he wanted was to be able to get out of this thing that was making so much noise and back to Granny Thelma and his home. Eventually he stopped crying and decided to put on a brave face. His eyes were becoming accustomed to the dim light and he could make out the front of the old settee, so he jumped onto it and lay down.

Surely the big man would open the door soon he thought to himself and then he would be able to run back into his house.

"As soon as I get into my house" he said to himself "I will try out the new settee to see if it is as comfortable as this old one," but, before he could think of anything else the "room" he was in started to shake. Sparky was

7

thrown to the floor with a bump and he had trouble trying to stay on his feet. This lasted for a very long time as Sparky as Sparky continued to try to stand up.

Suddenly the "room" stopped shaking and it became very still and quiet. He heard a noise similar to the noise he had heard when the door was locked and so he hoped that this time the door would open. "If it does" he thought to himself, and believing that he was still outside of his house "I will run as fast as I can through the gate and go and stand by Granny Thelma so that I will be safe".

As the door opened he sprang from the lorry and ran as fast as he could and only after a little while and realising that he was not where he had expected to be, he stopped to look around.

It was getting dark and it was beginning to rain as he looked at what lay around him and he could see very little. "What has happened and where am I" he thought "and, where is my home and Granny Thelma" "Come here" shouted the big man "I won't hurt you".

Sparky however was so alarmed that he turned and ran even faster.

The man stopped yelling and went back to his lorry, emptied the settee from the back, closed the doors, got into the front and drove away.

Sparky stopped after a while, just in time to see the lorry that had brought him here, disappear into the dark.

Now he could feel himself begin to panic. The rain was coming down harder. "I had better find myself somewhere to hide from the rain" he said and seeing a large box lying on its side, he ran into it and shook himself to get rid of some of the rain from his fur.

Looking out from the box he could see very little and so feeling very tired, cold and afraid he lay down to rest. "I will wait here until the rain stops and it gets light again and then I will find my way back home" he thought.

"What will I do if I cant find my way home and I don't ever see Granny Thelma again" he said. He tried to sleep but could not so he lay down in the box and began to cry.

Granny Thelma waved goodbye to the men who had delivered her new settee and who were taking the old one to the rubbish tip for her and went back inside. She decided to make herself a cup of tea so she went into the kitchen and put the kettle on to boil. Looking out of the window she noticed that it was beginning to rain and was getting rather dark.

She made a cup of tea and walked into the living room expecting to see

Sparky curled up on the new settee but to her surprise he was not there.

She shouted for him to come but he was not in the house.

She went out into the garden shouting Sparky's name but he still did not come. She went into the house and put on her coat and then went back outside calling Sparky's name continually but still he did not come to her. She opened the gate and looked around but now the rain was pouring down heavily and she could see nothing as the rain went into her eyes, so she ran back into the house and taking off her wet coat she went back to the door again and continued to call his name. "Where are you" she shouted loudly "Sparky where are you".

Now she was really worried and began to cry loudly "O Sparky where are you". She continued to shout long into the night but Sparky did not reply.

Chapter Three……..Sparky Meets the Cat Gang

When it was light enough to see, he looked around and was amazed to see

hundreds of rubbish bags like the ones that Granny Thelma would leave

for the rubbish lorry. Then lorry's began arriving and leaving more

rubbish.

"Where does this all come from" he thought to himself "Granny Thelma

never had this many bags before" thinking that she was the only one who

threw away rubbish and that the men came to the house just to collect it

from her but never knowing why.

Suddenly he spotted his old settee in the distance. It was covered in a

large piece of cardboard that must have blown up onto it during the night,

but he recognised it and remembering his toys he ran over to where it was

and jumped onto it and, thinking only of his toys, he did not notice a

bundle of fluff lying curled up in a ball on one side of the settee and

hidden by the cardboard.

As Sparky jumped onto the settee the bundle of fluff leaped into the air

and started to hiss very loudly which startled Sparky who in return started to growl and bark as loudly as he could.

The bundle of fluff was a cat, who had been sleeping on the settee.

Sparky, who had never seen a cat before was mystified as to what this

thing that hissed at him was, so he barked and barked which made the cat

hiss and spit all the more. As the cat hissed and Sparky barked, Sparky

had the chance to look at this thing that stood before him.

It was furry like him, the fur being a mixture of shades of grey.

It was about the same size as him but its nose was not pointed like his.

Also, it had a black patch over its right eye which made it look really

scary. Sparky noticed also, that he only had a short tail.

"Are we going to stand here all day barking and hissing at each other, or

are we going to stop now" said the cat and Sparky who was still quit

bewildered said" well I will stop if you do" so they both stopped .

"W, W, what are you?" said Sparky nervously "and where do you come

from and what are you doing on my settee".

"I am a cat" was the reply "and anyway I have been here longer than

you, this is my home, so how can this be your settee, this is mine, I was

on it first of all" said the cat firmly. "this is my settee".

"But it is mine and all of my toys are inside" replied Sparky "and anyway, who are you" he added.

"My name is Nelson" was the reply" "and if this is your settee, what is it doing here" he asked "and where are your toys?".

Sparky went to the rear corner of the settee and with his teeth he pulled back the old worn out cushion so that Nelson could see the toys.

"I am here because I am lost" said Sparky, "I went to rescue my toys from the back of a big moving box like the one over there" at the same time he pointed to a lorry that was dumping rubbish "and I became locked in and when the doors opened again I was here and I just want to go home" he added as the tears began to fill his eyes.

"Don't start crying" said Nelson "why don't you just go home" he asked?.

"Because I don't know where my home is" replied Sparky and this made him realise how much he was missing Granny Thelma and his home, so he started to tell Nelson how he came to be here, and all that had gone before.

"What is this place and why are you here and why do you have that patch over your eye?" asked Sparky.

"I was in a fight with an enemy and my eye was damaged and I can no longer see out of it so I wear this patch to stop others staring at it and to keep it clean and I can focus better with the other eye when it's on, also this is the place where all the rubbish that people don't want is brought to" said Nelson "and it is my home and the home of the gang".

"Gang" asked Sparky "what's a Gang?

"A gang is a group of friends who hang out together and play and look after each other" replied Nelson "and I am here because this is my home, I was born here" he added.

"Don't you have a Granny Thelma"? asked Sparky.

"No, Tigger is the boss around here" said Nelson.

"What is a Tigger"? asked Sparky.

"Goodness, you ask a lot of questions" said Nelson. "Well Tigger is a cat like me but bigger and very clever and he teaches us how to find food and how to do other things as well" replied Nelson and then he started to tell Sparky about the rubbish tip and how it was and always had been home to the Cat-gang.

He told Sparky of the many fights there had been between the Cat-gang and the Rat - gang as they all tried to find food amongst the rubbish and how Tigger had always led them and taught them how to survive and to help each other.

Suddenly Sparky started to growl loudly which surprised him because he did not normally growl, but today he had done so twice.

Nelson saw that Sparky was looking past him at something on the settee and looking behind him Nelson saw a rat who, afraid at the sight of Sparky,(having never seen a dog before) suddenly decided to run.

It had in fact been a large rat and being an enemy of the Cat- gang had intended to creep up on Nelson, bite him as hard as he could and then run back to the rat hideout, but now that he had been seen, he ran off quickly and without doing any harm.

"That was one of the rat-gang who live here as well" said Nelson "but they are our enemies, they want the dump for themselves and try to attack us whenever they can but you were very brave" he said to Sparky "they have very sharp teeth and could have done me a lot of harm if you had not scared him off, that means I am in your debt and if you ever need a favour or a friend I will be there for you.

"I did not know what it was so I just started to growl because it was scary" Sparky said, whilst at the same time feeling pleased that he had made a friend. He was sure that he would need a friend if he was going to find his way back home.

They heard a noise behind them so they turned around quickly thinking that the rat had returned but it had not.

"There comes Tigger and the gang"said Nelson and, as Sparky turned he saw a group of Cats approaching. The first cat Sparky saw was Tigger and he was very big indeed, even bigger by a small amount than Sparky himself. He walked very upright and this made him look even bigger.His fur was a shiny silver with darker stripes "he does look clever" thought Sparky.

After him came a small greeny grey cat who was much smaller, "My name is Puddy" she said to Sparky.

Then came a black cat who was bigger than Puddy. "My name is Blacky" he said and Sparky noticed that his eyes stayed wide open as if he were staring. After him came another black cat and Sparky saw that she only had half a tail "my name is Sooty" she said.

 Last of all came another green grey cat called Fred but he was thinner. He looked about all of the time as if he were expecting something to happen but Nelson told him later that he was always watching out in case the rats tried to creep up on any member of the Cat-gang.

"Who is this and what is a dog doing on our patch" asked Tigger in a strong deep voice.

"My name is Sparky" Sparky said loudly as he tried to make himself sound unafraid "and I am lost" he added.

Nelson told Tigger everything that Sparky had told him and also told Tigger how Sparky had scared off the rat and thereby stopped him from getting hurt.

"I see" said Tigger. "and how do you intend to get home if you don't know the way" he asked "you cant stay here, our enemies will think we are getting soft if we allow a dog to stay."

"You are very wise" said Nelson to Tigger, "can't you think of something".

"Well he did save you from the rat" said Tigger "let me think for a moment" and he began to pace up and down mumbling to himself.

Chapter Four.....Plans are Made

After a while he stopped and, looking firstly at Nelson and then at Sparky he said "I have decided, that because Sparky saved you from harm, and that it is plain to see that he will never get home without any help, that you Nelson will help him to find his way home".

"It can't be that difficult and after you have taken him home you can come back again. Yes that is how it will be" he said.

Nelson looked at Tigger with a puzzled expression. "How will I know which way to go"? he asked "how will I know where to start"?

Sparky in the meantime was feeling quite excited. Having someone to help him find his way home made him feel better. He liked Nelson and he felt sure that with Tiggers guidance, the two of them would find the way back to Granny Thelma.

"Yes" said Tigger "that is a very good question" and he began to pace up and down again just as he had done earlier.

A short while later he said to Sparky," When you go out in the morning and you look up into the sky, is the sun at the front of the house or the back"? he asked Sparky.

Not expecting such a question, Sparky had to think for a moment. "Well" said Sparky "when I go into the back garden the sun is in front of me, well I think it is" he added.

"THINK" shouted Tigger loudly "YOU THINK! HOW CAN I HELP YOU IF YOU DON'T KNOW"? and then seeing that he was scaring Sparky he lowered his voice and said "it is very important that you know where the sun is in the morning for only by knowing that can I send you both In the right direction".

"Well, yes" said Sparky nervously "I am sure that the sun is in front of me, but why is that so important?" he asked.

"Quite simple" replied Tigger, "you must walk with the sun behind you in the morning and with the sun in front of you in the afternoon and that way you will be at least heading in the right direction".

"I don't understand why" said Nelson to Tigger. "Goodness" said Tigger "if you walk with the sun behind you in the morning then you will be walking in the direction of Sparky's back gate, not directly towards it but at least in the right direction."

"When Sparky comes out of his house in the morning the sun is in front of him and shining onto his house so when Sparky turns around and faces his house the sun is behind him, do you understand now"? he asked them and they both answered "yes" in unison.

"My"! Sparky thought to himself, Tigger really is clever as he gazed at him "I was so lucky I found Nelson and the Cat-gang."

"But before you leave we must find you some food so that you are not hungry " he said and told the rest of the gang to go search for some food for them all.

Puddy, Sooty, Blacky and Nelson ran off and started to look amongst the rubbish for any food that had been thrown away but Fred went to a high mound and kept an eye open.

Tigger, who was the leader did not have to search, the others searched for him.

"Why is Fred standing up there"? asked Sparky.

"So that he can keep watch whilst the rest of the gang search" replied Tigger "when they are searching they cannot keep an eye out for the Rat-gang who may be lurking" he added.

"Another sign of Tigger's cleverness" thought Sparky to himself as he looked at him with admiration.

It took quite some time for the cats to find enough food to feed the whole gang but eventually they found enough so they all sat on Sparky's old settee and shared the food between them.

 There were pieces of fish and a variety of different things. When they had all finished Tigger looked around and said "it is getting dark now, much to dark to start a journey, so I suggest that we all remain here and then Sparky and Nelson can leave in the morning, by then it will be light, the sun will be out, and you will be able to plan the way you are going to start"

"I am looking forward to leaving and to getting home but what about my toys"? he asked

"Well" said Puddy, rather surprising herself at her sudden outburst and causing everyone to look at her, "you can't take them all with you".

"I realise that" answered Sparky "but I will miss them, I have had them for so long and Granny Thelma gave them to me".

"Even one toy would be to much to take on what might be a long trip" Sooty said, thinking that it was time that she joined in "why don't you just take a small toy or part of one as a keepsake and maybe, once you have found your way home, you could remember the way and come back for them with Granny Thelma".

"How would I explain to her that I wanted her to come here with me to collect them" he replied " I think that I will have to leave them here but your idea of taking a part of one is an good one".

So Sparky went to the corner of the settee where the toys were hidden (disturbing Fred who had made himself comfortable there and who gave a disgruntled moan of annoyance) and looked them over. "What shall I take"? asked Sparky to no one in particular.

"Which of the toys is your favourite" asked Tigger.

Sparky looked over all of the toys that were there and then pointed to a soft teddy bear that was dressed in a green top and blue trousers and which had a red bandana around its neck. "That one is my favourite because it is soft and colourful" replied Sparky.

Tigger went over to the teddy bear, brushing Sparky aside as he passed him so that he had more room. Using his teeth he took hold of the teddy bear by the red bandana and started to shake it until the toy and bandana separated.

"There" he said to Sparky holding out the bandana, "put your head through the hole so that it drops over it and onto your neck".

This Sparky did and the bandana fell around his neck and rested on his shoulders.

"Well, I think we will look rather smart, you with your bandana and me with my eye patch" laughed Nelson and everyone else started to laugh as well.

All of the Cat-gang and Sparky cuddled up on the settee to rest, however, Fred slept with one eye open, always on the lookout for any of the Rat-pack, who may come to close.

In a far corner of the rubbish tip , in a group of tunnel's below ground lived the Rat-pack. There were a lot of them in all shapes, sizes and colours but the biggest of all was there leader.

Just after he was born his mother had heard one of the men who worked at the rubbish tip call to another man using the name "Herk" and liking the name she called her son Herk. Due to his size and scary face he had become the leader of the Rat-pack after the death of the last leader. There would normally have been a leadership contest but because of his size none of the other rats were brave enough to stand against him.

Although there were only a few cats living at the tip, Herk disliked them because they took food that he felt belonged to his gang, but mostly he disliked them because they did-not fear him and this angered him very much.

He would spend many an hour thinking of ways in which he might be rid of them, but as of yet he had not thought of a way.

His second-in-command was called Sneak because he would sneak up on the other rats from behind and scare them.

He did this only because he knew, that if the other rats tried to retaliate, then Herk would warn them off, although, he was not a coward, for it was he who had tried to bite Nelson before he was chased off by Sparky. The Rat-gang would spend the day searching for food and at night they would stay in their tunnels for warmth.

However there was always a lookout keeping watch outside and on this evening it was Sneak's turn.

Herk went outside to where Sneak was hiding and stood beside him.

"Anything happening" he asked Sneak.

"Nothing at all, it is quite still" replied Sneak "the Cat-gang and that other horrible thing that I told you about are very quiet, in fact, they are all asleep on that big bed thing (meaning the settee) and not one of them is on guard."

Herk felt an urge to rouse the rest of the gang and to raid the Cat-gang while they slept but he knew that the cat they called Fred, was always alert, and of course, there was also the other animal who had frightened Sneak earlier.

It did-not take long before the urge left him for he knew that he had to be sure that any raid he planed would work, for if it did-not, then he could loose face within the gang and there might even be a challenge to his leadership.

"What do you think that new member of the Cat-gang is" asked Sneak "and why has he joined up with them?" he asked further.

"I don't know, but they all seem very friendly to each other" replied Herk "but I am sure there is something going on, I just don't know what" he added.

After a while and sensing that Herk had become deep in thought Sneak asked him if he should call together some of rats and then try to sneak up on the group while they slept.

"Too risky" said Herk "we don't know if they really are asleep or if they are just pretending and waiting for us, let us wait for to-night and see what happens in the morning, I am a little tired now so keep watch until you are relieved and we will decide what to do then" and with that he turned and went back inside.

As Sparky awoke, he noticed that the settee was completely empty and looking around he saw the cats scurrying around, looking for food and for water to drink. "Why did you not wake me so I could help you search" he asked Fred who was perched upon his mound and was keeping watch.

"Tigger thought it would be best to let you sleep longer so that you would be ready for your journey" Fred told Sparky.

"But what about Nelson, he has a long journey too, why was he not allowed to sleep longer" asked Sparky.

"Nelson is used to getting up early when it is his turn to keep watch, so he does not need so much sleep, he is always alert, we are just making sure you are both fully fed and then when you are ready, you can begin your journey" explained Fred.

Realising that what Fred had said made sense, Sparky ran over to where the others were searching and after saying hello to everyone, he joined in with the search.

The Rat-gang were also out and about searching for food, all except Herk and Sneak. They were hiding behind a box ,watching the Cat-gang as they searched for food.

They saw the arrival of Sparky and noticed how he joined in the search.

"Very very strange" said Sneak to Herk, "I wonder what's going on, what are they up to".

"Yes indeed, it is very strange" replied Herk, "I think we should remain here and keep watch while the others keep searching for food. They can share what they find with us later, I need to know what's going on."

Sparky and the Cat-gang sat down and shared the food they had found between them although Sparky had a feeling, that he and Nelson were given a larger share.

He had intended to say something but he knew that the gang meant well and were only thinking of their journey.

His thoughts were interrupted by Fred's voice. "I think we are being watched by a couple of the Rat-gang" he said looking in the direction of the box behind which Herk and Sneak were hiding.

"Yes I was expecting them to take an interest in what we are doing" was Tiggers reply. "They are obviously worried by all the activity and the sudden appearance of Sparky".

"I am worried about leaving you alone. With only five of you here, the rats might get brave and mount a raid on you. Maybe we should wait a little longer, perhaps a few days or so just in case" said Nelson.

"No the sooner you leave then the sooner you return" answered Tigger sternly, "The sun has risen and you are well fed, it is time for you both to be on your way."

"But we can't leave you alone if there is any danger" said Sparky bravely not wanting to leave the remainder of the gang alone but at the same time wanting more than anything to be on his way. He did so want to find his way back home to his Granny Thelma and the warmth and comfort of their house.

"You must leave now, you must not wait any longer and no buts, I see clouds in the distance and if you don't leave now, the sun may become covered by them, and you wont have it's light to guide you, you must leave now" declared Blacky as he gazed into the sky.

"Blacky is right but take note of this" said Tigger "Do-not waste time when you don't need to, keep hidden when you can and remember to keep the sun in the right place at all times. Do you both understand"? he asked Sparky and Nelson.

"Yes, we both understand" they said in unison "but I still think we should wait awhile" added Nelson.

"Just get Sparky home safely and return as quickly as you can" Tigger said to Nelson and to Sparky he added "Nelson is wise to the ways of the land, well at least more than you are, so listen to him and do what he say's and Nelson you must remember also to leave marks on trees and anywhere else you can during your travels to use as markers to show you the way back once you have found Sparky's home. Now go and take care".

So Sparky and Nelson said their farewells to the rest of the Cat-gang and then, with the sun behind them, they started off on their journey to find Sparky's home, both wondering what lay before them.

Herk and Sneak remained hidden behind the box, looking at what was happening over at the Cat-gangs side of the rubbish tip.

"Two of them are leaving" Sneak muttered to Herk under his breath so as not to be heard by the Cat-gang "would this not be a good time to attack the Cat-gang while they are only a few, we could frighten them away forever and then the tip would be ours".

"No, not yet" replied Herk. This could be a trap to lure us out and then they could surprise us. No we stay hidden and only come out to look for food. We will wait until we know what is going on".

"We will have to keep watch just in case those two are leaving" Herk thought to himself. "Sneak is right, if they have gone then this could be the chance I have been waiting for, the chance for total domination of the rubbish tip.".

"Come let us go back into our tunnels" Herk continued "but we must send out a guard to keep watch. Arrange it and tell the guard to let us know if and when the other two come back. You and I will make plans, just in case they don't, just in case".

Chapter Five ……..The Journey Begins

Sparky and Nelson were very quiet as they left the tip, both deep in

thought. Would they find the way to Sparky's house, would the rest of the

Cat-gang be safe and many other thoughts that, at this time, had no

answers.

On reaching the outskirts of the rubbish tip, both Sparky and Nelson

stopped and looked back for one last sight of their friends, and then they

turned so that the sun was behind them and continued on their way.

The journey was rather quiet for a while with Nelson looking up to the

sky to make sure that the sun was where it should be and Sparky followed

loyally behind.

They came upon a small road which was used by the lorries that were

going to the tip.

"What is this" asked Sparky who had never seen a road before.

Nelson who was deep in thought jumped at the sudden question.

"Goodness you made me jump" nelson said "and what did you ask, I did

not hear you". Sparky drew nearer to Nelson and repeated the question to

which Nelson replied " This is a dangerous place. It is used by those big lorries going to the rubbish tip and sometimes they travel very fast and if you are not careful you could be knocked over and hurt. We may see a lot more of these roads so always stop and look. I have had a few narrow escapes myself".

"I will have to remember that" thought Sparky and having checked that it was safe to do so , they crossed the road and entered the field opposite.

Remembering to keep the sun behind them, they walked at a steady pace in an effort to get as far as they could before midday.

They chatted as they went with Sparky telling Nelson of his home and Granny Thelma and how she would play with him and feed him.

"It must be great to have your food given to you and not to have to search for it" Nelson said to Sparky "and to have a warm place to stay must be a great thing to" he added.

When Sparky had finished, Nelson began to tell Sparky about his life at the rubbish tip. He could remember only a little of his mother but she had left the tip one day and had never returned.

It was shortly after that when Tigger arrived and he ,being big and strong took over looking after the cats at the tipand so it was that the Cat-gang was formed and since then Tigger had looked after them, teaching them how and where to look for the best food, and how to keep lookout for any potential enemy, this mainly being the Rat-pack.

Sparky had not taken much notice of the land as they travelled but Nelson had remembered to scratch trees and posts so that he could find his way back.

Chapter Six.........Sparky and the Sheep.

They climbed a hill and at the top Nelson stopped to make a mark and

this gave Sparky the chance to look around.

"What are they" yelled Sparky, frightening Nelson as he concentrated on

marking the tree.

"What is what"? he asked Sparky. "Down there in that field, all of those

animals, are they all just like me"?

Sparky was looking at a lot of sheep in the field and having never seen a

sheep before he assumed that they were dogs just like him.

Nelson looked into the field that Sparky was staring toward and seeing

the sheep, Nelson told Sparky that they were not dogs.

"What are they then and what do they do"? enquired Sparky.

"It would be easier if we went to the sheep and then you can ask them

yourself" replied Nelson.

Without thinking, Sparky started to run down the hill.

"Don't run" shouted Nelson "you won't be able to stop", but Sparky had

already forgotten the promise he had made to Tigger to listen to what

Nelson told him, and so, full of excitement, he continued to run down the hill.

Ahead of him and across his path Sparky saw a large tree trunk and as he grew nearer he thought he would jump over it and then keep running until he came to the fence behind which the sheep were grazing and so, when he was near enough he took a large jump.

Behind the tree trunk and out of Sparky's sight there lay a smaller tree trunk and as he jumped the first one he landed on top of the second one. This tree trunk then started to roll forward and because he was going so fast Sparky found that he was unable to keep his footing and all of a sudden he slipped over and began to roll down the hill. He rolled for quite a way before he was able to gain any control and when he did he was on his tummy rolling backwards. At the bottom of the hill was a large but not too deep, puddle.

Eventually Sparky reached the bottom of the hill and landed on his back in the centre of the puddle with a loud 'splash'.

A little shaken he got to his feet and began to shake the water from his fur.

Nelson had watched all of this from the top of the hill "I don't believe it, I just don't believe it" he thought to himself.

When he saw that Sparky had come to a halt he shouted down to him "Are you alright? Are you hurt?.

"I, I'm ok" Sparky shouted back after he had shaken most of the water from his fur. "I don't feel any pain" he added.

Sparky then decided to get out of the puddle in which he was stood.

The smaller tree trunk had rolled slowly down the hill behind Sparky and had come to rest in front of him so he had to leave the puddle by walking backwards.

The puddle was quite near to the fence behind which the sheep were, and a few of them had come over to the fence to see what was happening and one of them had put it's head through the fence to get a closer look.

Sparky walked backwards out of the puddle until he bumped into something which made him stop.

Turning around he found that he was nose to nose with the sheep that had put it's head through the fence.

Being surprised the sheep let out a loud "Baaa".

Having never heard this sound before and being startled Sparky jumped backwards and right back into the puddle the he had just left and landed with another loud 'splash'.

He slipped over and landed on his back with his legs pointing towards the sky.

Nelson, who had watched the events below unfold, stood at the top of the hill shaking his head in disbelief.

"Does this dog have no sense at all" he thought to himself "Will he ever learn" and he started to descend the hill and move toward the puddle in which Sparky was lying.

When Nelson reached the bottom of the hill he walked up to Sparky who was sat in the puddle and said "Have you stopped playing about now and are you getting out of there"?

Sparky replied "I'm not playing about. I slipped and fell into this puddle". He then stood up and began to shake the water from his fur again.

Nelson was stood quite close to Sparky as were a few of the sheep on the other side of the fence and as Sparky started to shake, the water went everywhere.

Nelson screamed out "STOP" and jumped back to avoid the water. (Cat's do not normally like water.) and the sheep began to Baa!

Sparky stopped shaking at the sound of Nelson shouting and the sheep

Baaing.

Nelson went over to him and told him how silly he was to have run down the hill like he had, and that he was supposed to do as he was told, and if he did so they had more chance of arriving safely home.

"I will in future" he promised Nelson "I promise."

"I wonder" thought Nelson "I wonder".

Amid all the noise and confusion, none of them had noticed the arrival behind the fence of a very large sheep.

In a loud voice he asked "Who are you and what do you want here by my field and why are you upsetting my sheep.?

Sparky looked at this sheep. It was much bigger than all of the other sheep and it had two large pointed things sticking out of it's head.

"Well" replied Sparky " I have never seen animals like you before and I thought you were the same as me and I am called Sparky and this is my best friend Nelson and we mean you no harm and what are those things sticking out of your head"?

The large sheep looked at the two in front of him and realising that they meant no harm he said " My name is Ram and these are all members of my flock. I look after them and protect them and their babies when they are born and these are called horns and I use them to scare off any enemy who might want to harm my flock".

"I hope that he dose not think that I am his enemy" thought Sparky.

What is a flock" asked Sparky and, as if he were expecting the question and before Ram could reply Nelson answered "A flock is a gang that Ram looks after, just like the Cat-gang except that as you can see, a flock is a lot bigger than our gang".

"I see" said Sparky "but what do you do and what do you eat" he asked Ram hoping that Ram might give them some of his food. They had been travelling for quite a while and Sparky was beginning to feel hungry.

"We supply wool for the people to make warm cloths from. This is because they do-not have fur of their own so we give them ours and they make blankets and other things too."

"So that's where Granny Thelma gets all of her warm things from" thought Sparky as he thought back to the warm blankets on Granny Thelma's bed.

"But what do you eat"? Sparky asked and he was rather surprised when Ram told him that the sheep ate the grass in the field.

"GRASS" replied Sparky loudly "is that all you eat all of the time."

"Yes, well, most of the time. Sometimes we are given Hay to eat if there is not much grass in the hot weather but mainly we eat grass".

"What do you eat?" Ram asked Sparky and Sparky explained that Nelson and the Cat-gang would rummage through the bags and bins that were in the rubbish tip where Nelson lived but that he would be fed by Granny Thelma and that he was lost and that together, he and Nelson were trying to find Sparky's house.

"Who is this Granny Thelma" asked Ram so Sparky told Ram all about her and about his home.

"Now I know why you want to find your home" said Ram adding that he would do the same if he were lost and had such a nice home to go to.

"Well, if you go to the far side of that big field over there, you will see a big house. That is where the people who look after us live and I have seen some of the bins you speak of there .Maybe you will find something to eat in them and they also have a dog but much bigger than Sparky" Ram told them.

Nelson made a memory scratch for the return journey then he and Sparky thanked Ram and the flock for all of their help and started off across the field.

Chapter Seven ………Sparky Meets Brutus.

"We have been a long time talking to the sheep" Nelson said to Sparky

and we must not forget where the sun is".

Together they walked in the direction that Ram had shown them, both

feeling hungry and hoping that they would find some food soon.

As they came to the edge of the field they saw, ahead of them a very large

house with other buildings here and there.

Sparky noticed some large birds walking around and pecking at the

ground.

"Perhaps they will play with me" he thought to himself. "I could chase

them like I do to the ones at home but first I need some food".

Nelson had never before looked for food in bins which were outside of

houses.

The tip was the only place he had searched, and so neither he nor Sparky

thought that there would be any harm in searching through them and the

bags that they could see.

They walked over to the bins and Nelson began to claw at one of the bags, which seemed to have a nice smell coming from it, until it ripped open and the contents fell out.

Sparky meanwhile had noticed a smell coming from a bin that stood not too far from the bags. It was too high for him to see inside so he jumped into the air trying to see what was inside.

The bin was quite high so Sparky moved closer and then jumped forward but he knocked into the bin as he did so.

The bin fell to the ground making a very loud bang and causing all of the contents to fall out onto the ground.

From within the large house there came a loud barking sound and both Nelson and Sparky stopped and looked toward the house.

Coming toward them, running very fast came a really large dog who continued to bark as it ran.

"I don't think this dog is going to be too friendly" yelled Nelson "RUN" he cried and he ran to the nearest tree and climbed up into it as far as he could go.

Poor Sparky, who of course could not climb trees and did not realise that the large dog could mean him any harm was slow to re-act, not understanding why Nelson had shouted to run, and why he was now hiding up a tree, however, the loud barking did cause him concern and so, seeing a small hole in the bottom of a hollow tree not too far away, he ran as fast as his little legs could go.

He could hear Nelson's voice coming from the tree he was hiding in shouting "Run Sparky Run" and this made his little legs go just a bit quicker, quick enough to reach the hole and get inside before the large dog reached him.

The large dog stopped at the tree inside which Sparky was hiding and poking its nose as far as it could into the hole it continued barking. Sparky was very scared and shouted to the large dog to go away, but this caused it to push its head even further into the hole.

Above the barking Sparky could hear a voice shouting "Brutus come here now" and then the large dog stopped barking but stood with his nose toward the hole and growled a deep frightening growl.

The dog poked its nose back into the hole again and continued growling. "Come here now" Sparky heard the voice shout out again "Brutus get here now" so Brutus started to remove his head and, realising that if he stayed at the back of the hollow then Brutus could not reach him, Sparky jumped forward, nipped Brutus on the end of his nose and then jumped back to the far side of the hollow where Brutus could not reach him. Brutus let out a scream and became very angry and tried again to get his head back into the hole..

Looking out from the hole but staying well inside Sparky saw a man walk up to the dog and put it on a lead. He knew what a lead was because Granny Thelma used one on him sometimes when it was dark outside and they were going for a walk. This was so that they did-not get separated. "Stop making that noise" the man said to Brutus "It was most probably a squirrel or a cat that knocked the bin over" as if expecting the dog to answer "I will pick up the bin and tidy up when we get back from our walk" and with that the man and dog moved off away from where Sparky and Nelson were hiding and disappeared into the distance.

"Are you alright" Sparky heard Nelson shouting from the tree in which he was hiding, "they have gone now, it is safe to come out" so Sparky crawled out from the hole in the tree just as Nelson was climbing back down from his hiding place.

"Wow" said Nelson "That was a big dog. Thank goodness the man came and took it away, and the bin is still upside down. If we are quick we may be able to find some food before they return".

"Yes" said ,Sparky and he ran towards the bin "come quick and help to search. See if you can find anything to eat too".

Sparky began sniffing through the rubbish on the ground. A tin caught his eye. Granny Thelma would often empty the contents of a tin into his feed bowl and the food always tasted good so he put his nose into the tin and sniffed.

 The smell was very nice so Sparky pushed his nose further into the tin to try and reach the bottom but when he tried to get it from his nose he found it was stuck.

"What are you doing" said Nelson "you are meant to be searching for food, not playing with that tin".

"Um Uck" (I am stuck) was all that Nelson could hear.

"What" he shouted back to Sparky, "I cant understand you".

"Um Uck, Um Uck (I'm stuck I'm stuck) repeated Sparky and then started to shake his head in an attempt to remove the tin.

Nelson thought for a moment "Um Uck" what on earth can he be talking about as he watched Sparky shaking his head.

Then it dawned on him just what it was that Sparky was trying to say.

"You mean your stuck" shouted Nelson to Sparky who stopped shaking his head.

"Ats ot I head. Um Uck ("That's what I said I'm stuck") Sparky shouted back at Nelson.

Nelson shook his head in disbelief. "What did I do to deserve this" he thought to himself and smiled as he watched Sparky try to shake the tin from his nose.

Realising that shaking his head was doing no good, Sparky held the tin in both paws and holding it tight, he pulled his head from the tin.

Nelson stood and laughed as Sparky tried to lick the bits of food from his face.

"Well, that's one way to get food I suppose" he said to Sparky and then going over to where the bin had fallen over, he began to search for some food for himself.

After they had eaten, Nelson told Sparky that he had been very clever holding the tin by his paws so as to remove it from his nose and this made Sparky feel quite proud.

"We will make a gang member out of you yet" Nelson told Sparky.

"Even though it might take a long time" Nelson thought to himself smiling quietly.

Chapter Eight……..Sparky Makes A Special Friend.

 Sparky and Nelson ate as much as they could find and then resumed their

journey, feeling much better inside with their bellies somewhat fuller.

They travelled at a good pace with Nelson remembering to leave marks at

different places to remind him of the way back to the rubbish tip once he

had found Sparky's home.

The sun had long reached its full height in the sky and without Sparky

realising it, Nelson had changed direction so that the sun was in front of

them.

The two of them continued on their journey chatting merrily as they went

with Sparky asking Nelson lots of questions, some of which he could

answer, and others he could not.

It was beginning to get dark when Nelson suggested that it would be a

good idea if they found somewhere dry to spend the night.

Sparky wanted to continue but he did feel rather tired and he knew that it

made sense to rest.

They had been walking through a field and were approaching a wooded

area when they saw an old hut.

"Let's look in there" suggested Nelson and together they entered the hut.

The floor of the hut was dry and so it was decided that they should rest inside and continue their travels in the morning when the sun came up and they knew which way to go.

It was dark and they were both cuddled down and nearly fast asleep when they were disturbed by the sound of a cars engine.

Sparky felt that it was something smaller than the lorry that had taken him to the tip because the noise was much quieter but the memories that the sound brought back scared him a little anyway.

Nelson suggested that they remain where they were and this Sparky readily agreed to, so they remained inside the hut, but continued to look through cracks in the walls, and to listen out for other noises.

They saw a light moving through the wooded area in front of the hut, but further back inside the woods.

The light stopped for a short time.

They heard the sound of a door opening, and then after a short time, it slammed shut again, a noise that Sparky remembered all to well.

The lights began to move again, and after a short while, they disappeared completely and the silence returned.

"I wonder what that was all about?" asked Sparky but Nelson did not know so he recommended that they go back to sleep.

After a short time and just as they were beginning to fall asleep, they were disturbed again, but this time it was a different noise.

Sparky recognised the sound immediately because it was the sound of a dog barking and crying in distress.

Sparky was on his feet and looking into the woods in the direction from where the noise was coming.

Sensing that something was wrong with Sparky, Nelson asked him if he knew what the noise was.

"Yes I do" replied Sparky "It is the sound of another dog and it is in trouble. I must go and help it" and without another word Sparky began running toward the sound.

"O no" thought Nelson "Not again. There he goes running off without thinking what he is doing".

So Nelson started to run after Sparky as fast as he could, and calling for him to slow down, but as usual, Sparky was not listening.

Nelson managed to catch up with Sparky, and together they ran into the wooded area in front of them.

The sound from the dog which was crying became more distressful and this spurred Sparky and Nelson on.

After a short time, they came to a clearing and slowing down, they were surprised to see a small dog tied to a tree and that a fox was nearing it menacingly.

Sparky began to bark loudly to let the fox know that he was near, and then the bark changed to a deep growl as he got nearer.

Nelson began to let out a deep frightening hiss which, together with Sparky's growling, caused the fox to lose interest in the small dog and turn to look at the two animals that were racing toward him. It saw a small dog with his lips pulled back and showing his teeth.

Beside him came another animal that it did not recognise It was making a hissing sound that really was quite scary.

The fox looked at the two oncoming animals and then turned and ran into the woods away from the advancing Sparky and Nelson.

Seeing that the fox was running away, Sparky and Nelson came to a stop next to the small dog that was tied to the tree.

"Shall we go after it" asked Sparky.

"I don't think so" replied Nelson. "Let us see if the dog the fox was frightening is alright".

The dog that was tied to the tree looked at the two animals that had frightened off the fox. She had seen a cat before and so knew what it was. Then she looked at the dog. She noticed that he was about the same size as her and had a friendly face.

Sparky and Nelson approached the dog. Sparky, seeing that she was tied up went behind her and started to bite at the rope that held her tied.

"O thank you so much, I have never been so scared" she said to them with tears in her eyes.

"You are safe now" said Nelson "but why are you tied to the tree" Nelson ask the dog "and what is your name".

"My name is Phoebe" (FeeBee) she replied "and I don't know why I was tied to the tree. I used to live in a place with my family and lots of other dogs and I was quite happy and then one day a man and lady came. They had a small girl with them. They took me away from my family and the other dogs and we went to the place were they lived. It was alright but the little girl kept pulling my tail and hurting me so one time I barked at her. The man shouted at me, tied me to this rope, drove me here and left me as you find me".

Sparky had been listening to what Phoebe was saying, but could not say anything himself due to the fact that he was still trying to undo the knot. "That is terrible" said Nelson and he continued "I have heard of that happening before to other animals when they are no longer wanted. Some of the cats and dogs that I have met on my travels have had the same thing done to them. It really is so sad but never mind. You are safe now". Sparky managed to remove the rope just as Nelson stopped speaking.

"Thank you so much for helping me and for untying me" she said to the both of them "but what are you doing here and what are your names." Nelson began to tell her of how he had met Sparky and of the journey they were on and why he and Sparky were in the wood together.

As Nelson was speaking Sparky took the opportunity take a closer look at Phoebe.

She was about the same size as him. She did not seem to have much fur and what fur she did have laid very tight to her skin. It was almost the same colour as his fur but with a little bit of green mixed in. She had small pointed ears and a short nose. Her eyes were quite large and all in all Sparky thought she looked rather nice.

While Nelson was telling her of his and Sparky's adventures, Phoebe look at her two hero's.

Firstly she looked at Nelson and noticed that he was as big as she was.

She noticed his colouring, his height but most of all she noticed the short

tail and patch over his right eye. She was tempted to interrupt him and ask

about it but felt that it might be rude at this time.

Then she turned to look at Sparky while at the same time taking in what

Nelson was saying.

She realised that there was nothing about him that she did not like. Even

the red scarf around his neck looked really nice. "He is so handsome" she

thought to herself and then feeling a little embarrassed and afraid that

Sparky might notice her attraction to him, she concentrated on what

Nelson was saying.

When Nelson had stopped speaking, Sparky asked Phoebe what she

intended to do now that she had nowhere to go.

"I am not sure what to do now" she replied looking at Sparky and Nelson

with a rather sad expression.

Before Sparky had even opened his mouth, Nelson knew just what he was

about to say and he was right.

"Well" said Sparky "You could join us. It would be better than being alone and it would be safer too" he added. He hoped that Phoebe had not noticed the excitement in is voice.

"Would that be ok with you Nelson"? she asked. She had wanted Sparky to make her such an offer. She felt drawn to Sparky and felt that he quite liked her too.

Noticing the bond that there seemed to be between Sparky and Phoebe, Nelson agreed that it would be a good idea if Phoebe did join them. It would be safer and he knew that it was what they both wanted, and so he suggested that they all return to the old hut so that they could try to get some sleep before they continued their travels.

The following morning, the three friends prepared to set off again. Nelson marked the hut and a few trees nearby and then, making sure that the sun which was just visible through the clouds was behind them, he started off back into the woods in which they had found Phoebe.

The three friends continued their journey happily chatting to each other. Nelson told Phoebe how he came to lose an eye and half of his tail and that the eye patch had been found at the rubbish tip that was his home. Sparky told her about Granny Thelma and of his home and how he came to be lost.

He explained to her about making friends with Nelson and the Cat-gang and about Tigger who led the gang and of the other members. He told her also of how it came about that he wore the red scarf around his neck. After a while, Nelson asked Sparky if he had said enough and was going to give Phoebe the chance to tell about where she had lived before she was taken away and what were the animals like at the place where she had first lived.

"I don't mind listening to Sparky" said Phoebe rather quickly and then wondering if she had spoken too soon.

 She did like Sparky and was enjoying his company but hoped that she was not making it to obvious. Of course, she was glad that Nelson was there too but she thought that Sparky was rather special.

"I have to put up with Sparky not listening to what I say and running off when he should not" muttered Nelson to himself "and if that is not bad enough I now have to put up with this romantic stuff".

Phoebe began to tell of how she had been born at the dog pound and of her parents and brothers and sisters.

"Some of my brothers and sisters were taken away before I was" she began "and now that I know what happened to them I hope that they are alright and did not get tied up as I was."

"I have heard of these places where people collect animals from to take home but in most cases they stay there and are very happy so I guess that you were just unlucky." Nelson told them.

That made Phoebe feel much better knowing that her brothers, sisters and friends were most probably quite happy now, and so the journey continued with lots of talk, but with Nelson remembering to check where the sun was and to make marks every so often as they went along their way.

Chapter Nine…………….The Angry Bull.

The three friends travelled on their way, laughing and joking as they went. Nelson noticed that Sparky and Phoebe were becoming quite close which he thought was rather fun and good for them both, as it helped them to forget what they had been through.

They crossed many fields, lanes and streams, where they would rest and take a drink.

After some time they came to a field which was surrounded by a large wire fence. On either side of them were trees and bushes which meant that the only way forward was through the field.

Looking through the fence they saw some very large animals. "What are they" Sparky asked Nelson.

They are called cows" replied Nelson and they supply the people with milk to drink.

"They are very big" remarked Phoebe "are they friendly"? she asked.

"I don't really know" replied Nelson, "I don't know much about them. I only heard about the milk from a cat that came to the tip one time. He told us that he used to live on a farm where there were cows and other animals, and that he had seen the cows giving milk. When we asked him why he was no longer at the farm he said that he had been driven out by younger cats, so he stayed with us for a while but then one day he was gone. We never did know what happened to him."

"How very sad that he was driven out of his home. Do all cats do that?" asked Phoebe.

"No, not at all" answered Nelson. "The cats that live at the tip, live there for ever and are happy to do so".

Before either Nelson or phoebe could say another word, they heard Sparky going "O! O!".

"What is it"? asked Nelson.

"Look" said Sparky, as he nodded at something happening in the field. Both Phoebe and Nelson looked toward the direction that Sparky was nodding in and they saw a few of the cows, who had noticed the three friends, were coming toward them for a closer look.

"Who are you and what do you want"? asked one of the cows.

Phoebe had noticed that the cows were female and so, before either of the other two could say anything and believing that it would be better if she did the talking, she proceeded to tell the cows of there adventure.

The cows listened quietly and when Phoebe had finished they wanted to know what the friends wanted at the cow field.

Phoebe explained to them that they needed to get to the other side of the field and asked if it would be possible for them to cross.

"Well, we won't mind" said one of the cows "but I am not so sure about Bull".

"Who is Bull" they asked in unison.

"Well" said the cow, he is the leader of the herd and he takes care of us and keeps us safe" she told them.

"Where is he"? they asked and the cow told them that he was at the top of the field. Together they put their heads through the fence and looked toward the top of the field. They saw an animal that looked like the ones that they were talking to but this one was much bigger. Not only was he bigger but he also had big horns on the top of his head and a ring through his nose. He was eating grass and they noticed that every now and then, he would snort through his nose.

"He looks rather angry" Nelson pointed out. "Do you think he will mind if we just run across the field quickly".

"That is what I would do" answered one of the cows.

"Wait until he is not looking and then run across as fast as you can".

At the top of the field, Bull was eating grass when out of the corner of his eye, he noticed some of the cows gathering together by a part of the fence. He was just about to yell out to ask what was going on when one of the cows moved enough to one side for him to see the two dogs and the cat.

"What do they want"? he thought to himself and started off down the field toward the gathering.

The three friends crept under the fence ready to start running. They said goodbye to the cows, took one last look toward Bull and then started to run.

As they did so Bull was starting to gather speed.

As they were running, Nelson looked toward Bull and saw that he was coming toward them at great speed.

"What are you doing in my field" Bull shouted as he ran toward them.

"Get out and leave my herd alone" he yelled.

"That is what we are trying to do" thought Sparky as the fence on the other side of the field grew nearer.

He looked toward Phoebe and Nelson to see if they were keeping up with him and was pleased to see that they were.

Bull was getting closer now, so much so, that they could feel the ground vibrating as he got closer.

Bull realised that if he kept going at this speed, he would not be able to stop before he reached the fence, and so reluctantly, he slowed a little, and this enabled the three friends to reach, and get through the fence.

Bull saw that he was not going to catch them so he stopped ,and snorting out of his nose he yelled to them to go and never come back.

Phoebe thought that he was very rude and so, as soon as she had got enough breath back, she walked toward the fence near to where Bull was standing, glaring and snorting at them and said "But we only wanted to cross your field and we mean no harm".

"I don't want you near my field again" he shouted and he banged against the fence with his horns. Go away and don't come back, I don't want to see you here again."

"Let's go before he becomes even ruder" said Phoebe and so they turned and moved away from the cow field.

Bull turned and grinned at the cows that stood nearby. "I think they will be alright and the little lady is not afraid to stand up for herself, I like that." he said to them and then walked away to continue eating the grass. The cows looked at each other in disbelief, Bull being nice, that's a first and together they laughed and then grinning to themselves, they too walked away and continued to eat the grass.

Chapter Ten…Frog, Hedgehog and Owl.

Moving away from the field, the three friends carried on their travels.

Phoebe mentioned to Sparky that she was beginning to feel hungry and

Sparky agreed that he to was somewhat hungry.

Nelson was busy marking a tree but when he had finished he did agree

that it was time that they found some food.

Nelson also mentioned that the sky was getting cloudy and that the sun

was beginning to disappear.

"It won't be long until I won't be able to find the way so we will have to

find somewhere to rest" he told them.

After a while , they came to a small stream where they stopped to drink

some water.

They were about to start walking away after satisfying their thirst, when

they heard a strange sound.

"Croak Croak" was the sound that they could hear.

They listened carefully to try to determine from where the sound was

coming.

"Look over there" said Nelson so Sparky and Phoebe turned their heads to where Nelson had observed something.

The three friends walked over to where two small animals were stood.

The first animal they saw and the one that was making the noise was a frog.

It was green and bumpy and when it croaked it's throat seemed to swell up.

The other was a little bigger than the frog. It was brown with a small head and had a pointed nose.

It's fur was quite wiry, even more than Sparky's was.

Nelson, who was closest said hello and never having seen such creatures before asked them who they were.

"Hello I am Barry and I am a frog and this is my friend Sadie. She is a hedgehog. We want to get to the other side of the stream which is easy for me but the water is to deep for Sadie."

"I can help you across" said Phoebe "I will pick you up gently in my mouth and carry you across" she said.

"Thank you very much for your offer but I don't think that that would be a good idea" replied Sadie.

"O, but why not" enquired Phoebe.

"Well it is because my fur is very sharp, like needles and you would hurt your mouth" Sadie explained "I use my needles to protect myself if ever I am in danger" she continued.

Phoebe went nearer to Sadie and felt her fur with her paw.

"Ouch you are right, they are sharp, thank you for telling me" said Phoebe.

After a little thought Sparky asked Sadie if she thought that she would be able to climb onto his back if he laid down first.

"I think I could" Sadie replied "But what is your plan?" she asked.

 "Well, if you climb onto my back and hold on tightly, I could walk across the stream with you on my back and then let you off on the other side."

"That would be wonderful" Sadie replied and so Sparky laid down as flat as he could and then Sadie climbed onto his back.

Walking slowly, Sparky crossed the stream and when he was safely on the other side, he laid down again so that Sadie could climb off.

Barry, croaking as he went, much to the amusement of everyone, hopped across the stream and stopped next to his fiend Sadie.

He and Sadie then thanked Sparky and asked why the three of them were at the stream.

"We stopped for a drink from the stream before we continue our journey" Nelson told them.

"Where are you travelling too" asked Sadie "Maybe we can help you just as you helped us" she told them.

"We are trying to find the way to my home" Sparky said and he told them of how he had become lost and of how he had met Nelson, the Cat-gang and Phoebe " we have to follow the sun but it has disappeared and so now we will have to wait until we can see it again before we can continue searching" he added.

"Have you asked Barney" enquired Sadie "he may be able to help you" she said.

"Who is this Barney and where do we find him"? asked Nelson "and how might he know".

"Well" Sadie began to explain, "Barney is an Owl and Owl's are the wisest of all living things and if anyone can help you find your way home, I am sure that he can."

"Where do we find him then?" asked Sparky excited that there may someone who might know a way of getting home soon.

"Barney is a night creature so you will have to wait until it is dark. He normally sits up there on the branch of that big tree" Barry explained.

"Well, it is no good trying to go anywhere at the moment because the sun has gone, so we may as well wait here, and speak to this Barney when he comes out" Nelson remarked.

"We will have to leave you here and be on our way" Sadie told them "we hope that Barney is able to help you find your way home and that you get there soon" and with that Sadie and Barry said their farewells, thanked the friends for there help in getting Sadie across the stream and then they turned and walked away.

Sparky, Phoebe and Nelson watched them until they had disappeared from view.

Nelson suggested that they rest under the big tree until Barney the owl appeared and so they went to the tree and sat down close to each other to keep warm.

"We shall have to ask this Barney if he knows where we can find some food as well as asking if he can help us to find your house" Nelson told them and Phoebe and Sparky agreed for they too were feeling hungry.

They cuddled together for comfort and warmth and slept a little but the fact that they were hungry stopped them from sleeping too well.

It was quite dark when they were awaken by a strange noise which was something like a hooting sound.

"Hoot, Hoot" they heard and getting up and looking around they saw, in the tree, a large bird perched on the branch that Sophie and Barry had told them was where they would find Barney.

It was very large and fluffy , with a flat face, a small beak and it's eyes were slanted.

"Hello are you called Barney?" shouted Sparky thinking that the owl was asleep.

The owls eyes suddenly opened very wide and became large and staring. "Yes I am, what do you want and why are you shouting, I am not deaf nor am I asleep". he yelled back in a deep voice.

"I am very sorry" replied Sparky "but I did think that you were asleep and we need your help".

"Need my help, Need my help." he repeated "what for and who told you to come to me. Do you think I have nothing better to do than help every animal that comes by. I do have a life of my own you know" he told them rather abruptly.

"Please help us" Phoebe asked in a soft voice "Sparky is lost and we are trying to help him find his way home and also we are very hungry" she added "please can you help us."

Barney looked down at her. "She is very polite and gently spoken" he thought to himself," and they don't seem to be a bad bunch. I suppose I could try to help them if I can".

"Well, alright then, I will help if I can but tell me how you came to be lost and what you want me to do. However, I need to know your names first. Which one of you is Sparky, the one that is lost?" he asked.

Sparky pointed himself out to the owl and then introduced Phoebe and Nelson. Then he told Barney of everything that had happened since he had jumped into the back of the lorry.

Barney listen with interest as Sparky told him of the adventures that had passed and of how he had met first Nelson and then Phoebe. Sometimes he chuckled at the funnier parts but then became more solemn as he herd of the Rat-Gang and of Brutus. He laughed to himself when he was told of the encounter with Bull for he knew of him but knew that he was not as bad as he tried to make himself seem.

"Well first things first. Not far from here, I will tell you the way later is a small village and there you will find some dustbins and in them I am sure you will find some food , but be careful of the tins, they can get stuck to your nose" and he chuckled as he remembered hearing Sparky tell of his earlier experience's with a tin.

"Now to the question of finding you your home, that is not so easy but from the description that you have given to me, I think I might have an idea of where it is, but I need to be sure. I suggest that the three of you go to the village and search for food. I will fly around for a while and I will meet you back here later" he added.

Sparky could not believe what he was hearing and Phoebe and Nelson began to get excited as well.

"You know where I live, you can tell me how to get there. How long will it take, when can we leave" he asked without taking a pause to breath.

"Slow down, Slow down" said Barney, "I told you that firstly I must fly around and check if I am right so calm down, the three of you do as I said and go try to find yourselves some food and I will see you here later."

Then he told them to follow a small trail that could be seen leading along side a field and which, after about a mile would lead to the small village, and without saying another word, he flew off into the darkness .

"I don't know if I want anything to eat, I am much too excited" Sparky

told Phoebe and Nelson but they insisted that he go with them.

"You will be ill if you don't eat and you are no good to anyone if you are

ill. We may have to travel a long way and you will need your strength

Phoebe told him and so, and realising that they were right, Sparky

agreed to join them in their search for food, and with that the three friends

set off in the direction that Barney had told them to go. After travelling

for a time, they saw the lights from the houses in the village not too far

ahead.

"I wish they were the lights from my home" remarked Sparky "I do so

miss Granny Thelma."

"If Barney is right and he does know where your house, is then it should

not be too long before we are there and you are re-united with Granny

Thelma" Nelson said to Sparky noticing that he was becoming impatient.

"You must wait until Barney gets back, come lets go and find some food"

Phoebe said. " Barney will be back soon and then we can continue our

journey to Granny Thelma".

Sparky knew that they were making sense and that they were thinking of

what was best for him, and so without further ado the trio walk toward the village. It did not take long for them to find some food amongst the bins and they were all able to eat their fill.

They finished eating and walked back to the tree to see if Barney had returned, but he had not, so the three friends huddled together for warmth and waited.

By now it was dark and they were feeling tired but all three were too excited to sleep and so they waited patiently for Barney to return with news.

Sparky thought of how Granny Thelma would react when she saw him again. Would she be angry that he had run off he wondered but he felt sure that she would be so glad to see him again that she would have no time to be angry.

Nelson was wondering about the Cat-Gang. Were they alright, had the Rat-Gang been making trouble, how long would it be before he could return to them.

Phoebe looked at her two new friends and hoped that she would be able to stay with them, especially Sparky, who she really liked.

If he found his home would Granny Thelma let her stay. Would Sparky want her to stay she asked herself although she felt that Sparky did like her as much as she liked him.

So deep in thought were they, that neither of them heard Barney return and did not know that he had returned to his branch until he hooted at them to gain their attention.

All of then jumped up in shock and looked up at the branch to see Barney perched there.

"You made us jump" Phoebe called up to him "We did not hear you come back."

"I know you did not hear me, that is why I hooted down to you" replied Barney.

"Did you find my home, did you find it?" asked Sparky urgently looking up at Barney and eagerly awaiting a response from him.

"Well now, that is the problem" replied Barney "the trouble is that a lot of the houses look the same, with gardens, trees and gates.

Sparky's heart sunk. He was so sure that today would be the day that he got back home. Nelson and Phoebe looked at him and could see that tears were starting to form in the corners of his eyes.

"Don't get down hearted just yet" said Barney who had also noticed that Sparky's head had dropped, "I think I know which house it is, going by your description of it and of Granny Thelma. As I flew over a short while ago, I noticed a lady fitting her description looking out of the back door of her house, so I am hopeful that I have found the right house for you."

Sparky and his friends became excited again and wanted to set off straight away but, on Barney's advice, as it was dark, they decided to wait until first light and to set off then.

Barney proceeded to explain to them, the way to go, to get to what he believed, could be Sparky's house.

There was in fact, quite a way still to go, but if they followed his route they would get there by evening the following day.

They would have to go across a lot of fields and a few roads, and there would be a few hills to climb in fact, he told them, the last big hill that they would climb was he hoped the one that looked down onto Sparky's house.

Nelson listened carefully for he was the guide, and he really did want to get Sparky home as quickly as he could so that he could return to the Cat-Gang. The three friends cuddled in again to wait for morning when they hoped they would find Sparky's house.

Chapter Eleven....Fred Raises the Alarm.

At first light the group roused and prepared to set off on their journey to Sparky's home.

Barney had remained in the tree to ensure that they had understood his directions.

Nelson, who had just finished leaving marks on a tree to show him the way back, assured Barney that he had understood. He repeated the directions to Barney to show him that he had remembered.

Barney then told them that it was time for him to go, so the friends thanked him for all of his help, said their farewells and then Barney flew away, hooting to them as he went.

So the group started off with Nelson leading the way and remembering as always to leave scratches on trees or other marks where they could be easily found. They chatted merrily about this and that as they went along and then at times became rather quiet as they went into their own moments of thought.

For quite a while they travelled with Sparky frequently asking Nelson if they were nearly there yet.

They eventually reached the bottom of a very large hill. Nelson suggested that they stop for a rest before they climbed the hill for he had noticed a large puddle from where they could all take a drink.

Sparky was about to protest for he felt an urge to climb the hill, (He had a feeling inside that he was not too far away and he wanted to get to the top of the hill as quickly as he could), when they all heard a voice calling, a voice that Sparky and Nelson thought that they recognised and so they all stopped.

"What is the matter and who is it that is calling.? asked Phoebe sensing that her friends had suddenly become very alert.

"It can't be Fred" said Nelson " he is back at the tip but it really sounds like him though."

Nelson had told Phoebe all about Fred and the other cats so she knew who Fred was.

Sparky agreed. "It sounds like one of our friends from the tip but if it is then what is he doing here, something must be wrong" he said with a hint of worry in his voice.

"Fred, is that you" shouted Nelson as loudly as he could and he was surprised to hear Fred calling back "Yes it is, where are you."

Nelson shouted back "We are here, just follow the sound of my voice"

and he kept on calling until Fred appeared from behind a group of bushes.

"At last, I have been searching for you for ages. Thank goodness you left

so many markers for me to follow, o, and who is this" he asked looking at

Phoebe. (When cats leave marks they also leave a smell and so Fred

knew that the marks were from Nelson because he recognised the smell)

Nelson quickly explained to Fred as to who Phoebe was but then wanted

to know why Fred had come looking for them.

"It is you I have come looking for. We need you back at the tip urgently. I

am also trying to find other cats to come and help as well. The rats seem

to be gathering and we fear an attack at any time. We could even be too

late now. We must return right away and at all speed." he told Nelson.

Sensing the urgently in Fred's voice, Nelson turned to Sparky and said to

him "I must go back. I am sorry but I am needed by my friends, and,

although we have become very close, they are my family and I must go

back with Fred before it is too late" he said.

 "We are nearly at your home I am sure. Do you think that you and

Phoebe will be able to manage the rest of the way alone"?

Sparky looked up at the hill behind him. He was sure that he was not far from Granny Thelma and home and he did so want to climb the hill to see if he was in fact right but these were his friends and they were in trouble.

"If you think that I am staying here you are mistaken, I am coming with you to help. That is what friends do, they help in times of trouble and I am coming with you" he said sternly to Fred and Nelson.

"And so am I" said Phoebe. "together we can frighten off the Rat-gang once and for all".

"Don't even try to stop us" Sparky told the two cat's, "as soon as Fred has rested, we should start back and go as quickly as we can."

Nelson looked at Sparky and gave a small grin. "Not so long ago he was like a small child and now look at him, giving orders to us."

"Ok, we all go as soon as Fred is rested." Nelson told them. "We all go together" and he felt quite proud of Sparky and Phoebe, especially Sparky, for Nelson also felt that they were not too far from Sparky's home.

Granny Thelma went to the back door as she had so often done since Sparky had disappeared. She looked across the fence and into the woods. Her eyes lifted to look up at the hill in front of her. She had had the feeling all day that Sparky was near and so she had come to the back door a lot hoping that he would be there, but he was not and so she would go

back inside, sit in her armchair and cry softly until she fell asleep.

Chapter Twelve…Sparky makes More Friends.

Once Fred had rested, the group started to travel back in the direction

from which they had originally come. Sparky turned to look back at the

hill, and wondered how long it would, be before he could return.

The return journey was easier because they had only to follow the marks

which Nelson had made. When they came to the tree where they met

Barney, they were surprised to see him on his branch.

"What are you doing here?" asked Sparky "i thought that you only

came here at night."

"That is normally correct" came the reply "but I could not sleep so I

decided to come here for a look about. What about all of you though, are

you not going the wrong way" he enquired.

"Well yes we are" answered Nelson but our friends are in trouble and

need our help, so we are returning as quickly as possible and will return

this way again when our friends are safe."

"Now that is highly commendable, especially when you may not be to far

from your destination. I hope you can help your friends and return before too long. I won't keep you so have a safe journey and I will see you all soon."

"Thank you. We will see you soon" they all replied and turned and continued on their way.

"Who was that"? asked Fred and Sparky began to tell Fred all about the journey so far and of the friends that they had made.Nelson was quick to point out to Fred the part about the tin on Sparky's nose and of how he had rolled down the hill and into the puddle.

Fred found the stories very amusing and the laughter was for him a short break from the worry he was feeling for his friends back at the tip.

They travelled on as quickly as they could having decided that they would not stop for too long even when it became dark but would continue throughout the night if the moon was bright enough to allow them to do so.

They became silent as the travelled, each caught up in their own thoughs and worries.

They passed the stream where they had met Saddie and Barry then later they stopped at the little village where they found food and they stopped for a short while to eat any food that they could find.

They were now rather tired and Nelson suggested that they rest for a while but Fred insisted that they should carry on.

"What good will we be if when we get back, we are so tired that we are of no use what so ever?" asked Nelson and Fred had to agree that Nelson was right, so after eating they stoped and had a short sleep with Fred and Nelson taking in turns to keep watch.

After a few hours and a well earned rest, the group re-started their journey. After some time they came to the field in which Bull and his herd of cows were kept. Making sure that he was at the top of the field, the friends crept across to the other side. A few of the cows saw them and smiled but they kept quiet so that Bull did not see them.

Some time later they passed the hut near the woods where they had rescued Phoebe, who, remembering her ordeal and feeling a pang of fear, moved closer to Sparky and continued the journey as close to him as she could get. This Sparky noticed and, as he liked having her close to him, he moved a little closer to her too.

Eventually they came to the field where they had met Ram and his flock of sheep and Sparky looked with embarresment when Nelson pointed out the puddle into which Sparky had twice fallen.

The sheep were in another part of the field and although Sparky would have liked to chat to them, he was glad that he and his friends could carry on uninterrupted.

After another few hours, they decided to take a short rest in a field before they finished their journey so that they would be refreshed when they arrived at the tip.

The field was on a slight slope which raised ahead of where they were all resting, and it was from the other side of the hill, that they first heard the noises.

It sounded as though a large number of dogs were charging toward them at speed barking as they ran.

The friends stood up and looked in the direction from where the noise was coming and not knowing if the dogs were friendly, they were very alert.

After a few moments, three dogs appeared over the crest of the hill, running, barking and playing happily together.

They did not notice Sparky and his friends at first and this gave Sparky a chance to look them over.

The first dog was similar in size and colour to him but it's nose was not so long, and it had no tail.

The second dog was much larger and very fluffy. The fur was white and grey. This dog had a very long tail which was very fluffy too.

The third dog was the same as the second dog but slightly smaller and it had no tail.

They played happily and Sparky relaxed and noticed that his friends were also relaxing.

The three playfull dogs came to a stop as they saw the group of animals below them.

"Hello" shouted the smaller dog "who are you and what are you all doing here?" the dog asked.

Nelson explained that they were there having a rest before continuing to the tip as quickly as they could. He explained why and that they were impatient to be on their way. He also told them the names of all in the group and he then asked them what they were doing.

"O, well we live here, this is where we play. Our owner is an artist who owns the land and she lets the cows and sheep roam around here sometimes, but we like to come here to run and play, and we sometimes stay out all night if we are enjoying ourselves" one of the larger dogs replied.

"What are your names? asked Sparky a little to the anoyance of Nelson who really wanted to move on.

"Well" said the small dog, "we are all called Kimmy and we call ourselves, one, two and three. This is because when our owner came and collected us from the puppy kennels she called me Kimmy and gave the other two different names but every time she called Kimmy, we all answered, so now she just calls for Kimmy and we all go to her. The tip you spoke of, is it the tip that is just a few miles from here?"

"Yes it is and we are in a hurry because our friends are in danger from the Rat-Gang and if we don't hurry we may be too late, and so it has been nice chatting to you but we really must go" said Phoebe who had noticed that the three dogs were female and, wanting to stop them from talking, she explained that she and the others needed to move on.

"RATS" exclaimed the three dogs together. "We don't like rats and you say that they are threatening your friends, well we can't have that can we ladies" the smaller Kimmy said. "We will have to come with you and give you some help if you would like us to, we love an adventure" she added, and the other two Kimmy's agreed.

"Well if you want to come and help, that would be really great, but can we please leave now" answered Fred, and so it was that the whole group set off together toward the tip.

Fred was pleased that they had found the dogs, for he had not been able to find some cats to come and help.

Chapter 13…...Back To The Tip.

They travelled on, only stopping now and then for a short rest, or to take a

drink from puddles that they passed and then, after some time they began

to recognise the scenery and realised that they were not far away now.

It was beginning to get dark when they eventually came to the small road

that they would have to cross to get into the tip and it was here that

Nelson called the group to a halt.

"We are nearly there now, we only need to cross the road" he said "we

don't know if our friends are safe and we don't want to let the Rats know

that we are back so we must be as quiet as we can".

Fred, being the quietest suggested that he go on alone to check that the

coast was clear. It had been arranged before he had gone to search for

Nelson and Sparky that Tigger and the remainder of the gang, would hide

on or near Sparky's old settee, and so Fred would look to see if they were

there.

With agreement from the others, Fred set out, crossing the road and

entering the tip as quietly as he could while keeping to darkened areas so as not to be seen by the Rat-gang.

Tigger heard a noise behind him, and turning quickly in case it was a rat, he saw Fred appear from out of the darkness.

"Thank goodness that you are back" Tigger said "Things are getting rather dangerous since you have been gone and Puddy has been injured" he added.

"What happened"? asked Fred alarmed to see Puddy lying on her side and obviously in distress with both Blacky and Sooty looking on worriedly.

"Well" answered Tigger "We went to look for food. I kept watch while the rest of the group searched. I heard a noise coming from behind me and it was a couple of the rats, so I chased them away but they were a decoy, and while I was chasing them, a few others attacked Puddy. Luckily, Sooty and Blacky were not to far away and went to her rescue, but one of the rats managed to bite her on the leg before they ran off, and now the leg is quite swollen".

"Did you manage to find Nelson"? asked Sooty.

"Yes and some other friends too" replied Fred. "in fact I had better go and get them before they get worried" he added and with Tiggers agreement, Fred went back to the entrance where he had left his friends.

Even Tigger looked surprised when Fred returned with Sparky and all of his new friends.

Fred quickly told Tigger and the cat-gang the story of how they had all come to be together, and that Phoebe and the three Kimmy's were going to help in the fight against the rat-gang.

"Now we have a chance" thought Tigger to himself and then he thanked Fred for finding Nelson and his friends so quickly.

Lucky was one of the Rat Gang who hated guard duty. Trying to stay awake for hours was something he hated and he would, once he thought all of the other rats were asleep, take a short doze himself.

"Nothing is ever going to happen here" he thought "and the rest of the cat gang won't return" so why should i bother staying awake and anyway, he allways woke up before the rest of the rats, so if he did have a quick nap no-one would notice.

Suddenly, he was awaken by a lot of noise and jumping to his feet he saw four large lorries entering the tip. Each lorry had a big piece of machinery on the back of it.

Lucky had never seen such things before and although he would never admit it to any of his friends, he was in fact quite scared.

"What is that noise?" came a voice from behind him and he turned to see

Herk, Sneak and a few other rats appear, for they too had been awaken by

the noise.

"O it is just some lorries entering the tip. Nothing to worry about" he

replied hoping that they did not notice the fear in his voice.

"Nothing to worry about" shouted Herk. "What's that over there then?"

and looking in the direction that Herk was looking, in and by the light

coming from the lorries, he saw that the Cat-gang had reformed, and, not

only that, but this time there were five dogs as well, two of which were

really large.

"Don't you think that that is something to worry about,why did you not

wake me, were you asleep"? he yelled.

"N, N, No I was awake all of the time" he replied in a scared voice (for

he had seen Herk when he was in a bad mood at other times and Lucky

knew how nasty Herk could sometimes be) "honest I was" he lied.

Herk glared at Lucky and was about to say something when the noise

from the lorries stopped and all of the lights went out.

"GO away all of you I need to think, I need to plan" he told all of the rats

and so, not wanting to make him angrier than he already was, they slipped quietly back into the tunnles that led to their homes.

"Think, think, think" he said to himself "I must come up with a plan to beat those cats and dogs, I must" and he fell into deep thought.

The new found collection of friends had decided to rest so as to be ready for what the new day might bring, and so they slept the little that they could, each taking in turns (except for Puddy who was not at all well) to keep watch.During Tiggers watch, he heard and saw a bit of movement now and then, so he remained very alert incase the rats decided to make a move.

"You had better all wake up" Tigger called to all of the group. "Things are happening" he told them as they roused from their sleep.

"Come and look" he said so they all got up and moved to look at what was causing Tigger to wake them.

Hundreds upon hundreds of rats had formed a circle around them, leaving just a small space near the exit.

The friends looked around in amazement, for they had never seen so many rats together in one place before.

"I think that we are in trouble" Nelson said quietly and the others agreed with him.

"I wonder why they have left a gap near the exit" asked Sooty.

"Yes, I wondered that too" replied Blacky.

"Maybe we are about to find out" said Tigger "look over there" and turning to look in the same direction that Tigger was looking in, they saw two of the rats begin to approach them.

Herk had thought long and hard. He knew that he had the chance to distroy the cats and dogs with his superior numbers but at what cost.

He would have been worried enough if it were only the cats that he was up against but now there were the dogs to consider as well, and two of them were really big, in fact bigger than any dogs he had ever seen before.

He was sure that he would win the battle if there was one, but he did not want to lose so many of his gang.

He had thought long and hard during the night and had decided on a plan that would rid him of the cats and not cost him the lives of any of his rat-gang.

Now that the first part of the plan was complete, namely the encirclement of his enemies, who were all together near the settee, it was time to put part two into operation, but this involved Sneak and him coming face to face with the cats and their friends.

Now, with his enemies surrounded, he and Sneak began the walk toward Tigger and his group.

"I wonder what they want" Nelson said outloud but to no one in particular.

"I don't know, but it will definatly be trouble of some sort" replied Tigger as the two rats came to a halt just a few feet away.

As the two rats came to a halt in front of him, Tigger asked loudly "What do you want and make it quick. We don't want you here".

"It has become obvious" began Herk "that this tip is to small for both gangs. We have the larger gang and would definitely win a fight, but there would be many losses on both sides. I am therefore proposing that you leave now and don't come back, thus stopping a fight. You and all of your group may leave through the gap that we have left behind you. If you refuse then lives will be lost on both sides".

"So, what is your answer"? asked Herk, "do we fight or do you leave"?

"Go back to your rats and I will give you our reply in a few minutes. I need to speak with my friends before I can give you an answer."

Herk and Sneak turned and walked back to where they had been standing to wait for a reply.

"My goodness" said Sneak "that was so clever. Do you think that they will leave?"

"Yes if they have any sence and then the tip will at last be ours" Herk replied.

Tigger thought deeply for a while.Everything that Herk had said made sence, but he was loath to give up the tip and to try to find somewhere else for all of them to live, but if he did not give it up, then there would be a lot of hurt, and this Tigger did not want. It was bad enough that Puddy was hurt he thought to himself.

"I think we should do as the rats say and move away from here" he said to all of his friends "there are too many of them, and a lot of us would be hurt or worse. I don't want to leave, but I think we will have to".

"We can't leave" the cat's said together. "we have lived here for ever, why should we go, where will we go?"

"We will find a new home I promise, but we can stay here no longer. Look how many of them there are. We would not stand much of a chance against them.We will stay together no matter what. Come it is time.I will let the rats know that we are leaving"

Sooty looked at all of her friends as they stood there with their heads bowed low, "Tigger is right" she said and although you don't want to admit it, you all know it too. We have had some good times here, but now it is time to move on and so we will but as we leave we will go with heads held high OK".

After a short while they all reluctantly agreed and so Tigger called to the rats to tell them that they were leaving.

When Herk heard Tigger call and say that the cat-gang and their friends were leaving, never to return he could not hide his excitement.

"Yes Yes Yes" he shouted "at last the tip is ours, we have won" and on hearing Herk yelling, the rest of the rat-gang began to cheer loudly.

The cats took one more look around at the place that had been their home for so long, and then, rather sadly, they moved together toward the exit, passing through the gap that the rats had left for them, and all the while as they went, the rats were cheering.

This angered Tigger very much but there was nothing that he could do, there were just to many of them and so leaving, although sad, had been the only option open to him. As leader of the cat gang, he had to do what was best for the gang, and he believed that he had made the right decision.

They walked through the gap, with the cheering from the rats still ringing in their ears as they neared the exit.

All of a sudden, the sound of the rats cheering was drowned out by a new much louder noise, which caused the friends to stop and look behind them.

They saw that the Machines that had been brought into the tip on the back of the lorries, had been unloaded and were starting to move.

"What sort of things are those"? asked Sooty "We have never seen things like that in here before".

"I don't know" replied Tigger "but I think we will soon find out" he added.

Puddy let out a painfull groan. "I will have to think of some way to help Puddy before she gets any worse" Tigger thought to himself, but his thoughts were interrupted by the movement of these new machines which he now noticed had flat fronts.

The machines started to move forward making a lot of noise as they did so.

"Look" shouted Blacky "They are flattening everything as they move along, the whole tip will be destroyed if they carry on".

"I think that that is what they mean to do.Have you noticed that none of the lorries that bring the rubbish have been here today, and normaly they begin to arrive very early. Maybe the tip is going to close anyway" Fred said and added that if that was the case, then what were the rats going to do.

At the same time that the cat-gang had been alarmed by the noise, the rats had also stopped to see what was happening.

The rats lived below the rubbish and travelled through tunnles to get to their homes.

Herk realised, that the tunnels would be destroyed if the machines carried on, and that any rats that were in them, would be hurt or worse, and it was his *intention* to warn the rats to run away from the tip and into the fields beyond.

Before he could do so however, some of the rats started to shout "Run Run" and within seconds the rats were running in all directions, alarmed by the noise and the shouting. Some ran into the tunnels thinking that they would be safe, but those who were nearest to the fields did in fact run into them and away from the tip.

Herk tried to warn the rats not to go into the tunnels, but when he called out he could not be heard.

He watched as the machines pushed the rubbish down until it was flat and he knew that many of his gang would perrish in the tunnels that were being destroyed.

As he looked around he saw the cat-gang and their friends watching from the safety of the firm ground near the exit and his anger raged.

He ran through the tip, dodging the machines untill he reached the place where the cat-gang were standing.

"I don't know how you did all of this, but you had better believe it ,I will get my revenge" Herk shouted at Tigger.

"I don't know what you are talking about, I had nothing to do with this" Tigger replied.

"You expect me to believe that. I thought it was strange that you would give up the tip so easily, you knew these machines were coming and that's why you were willing to leave. Remember this, I will be avenged" and with that he turned and ran back toward the rats on the far side, that had managed to escape from the machines.

Tigger turned to the friends and suggested that they carry on away from the tip before the machines came too near to where they were standing.

"Strange that Sneak did not come over with Herk.They always seem to be together. Maybe he was hurt by one of the machines" mentioned Sparky and the rest of the group agreed.

They moved away out of the exit and across the road to the safty on the other side.

Chapter 14..... The Way Home.

"What will we do now and where will we go?" Nelson asked and this was

something that they all wanted an answer to.

Tigger had been giving this some thought and he told the gang of his

plan.

"I promised Sparky that we would help him to find his home and that is

what we will do, and after that, we will have to see what happens" Tigger

told them.

"Granny Thelma will let you all stay with us, I know she will" Sparky

told them "just you wait and see" he said.

"We cannot join you" said the small Kimmy "our owner will start to

worry if we do not return soon. You are all safe now, and so it is time for

us to go."

"Thank you so much for joining us and for being willing to help" Sparky

said to them.

"We did not do anything really" the largest Kimmy replied.

"Maybe not, but you were willing to if it had been necessary, and that is a

sign of friendship" Tigger told them "and we all wish you well. Maybe we will meet again one day" he added.

"We hope so and we wish you luck on your journey to find Sparky's home, take care", said Kimmy 1 and with that the three Kimmy's ran off toward the fields, and back to their own home.

"Right then, I think we should start out to try and find Sparky's home as soon as possible" Tigger told them. "Then maybe Sparky's Granny Thelma will be able to help Puddy. She is looking really poorly now".

All of the animals agreed and so, with Nelson, (who by now was quite sure of the way back to where Fred had found them) in the lead, they all set off.

Sneak had been alarmed by the noise of the machines, as had all of the other rats, and, just kike them, he had run away from them as quickly as he could.

He found himself in a bush not far from the exit, and within hearing distance of his enemies who were talking together and had not noticed him and so it was that he overheard all that was being said.

When Tigger and group left the tip, Sneak searched frantically for Herk, and, when he found him, Sneak told him of the conversations that he had overheard.

"Well done" Herk said to Sneak "you have done very well indeed. Come we will round up the Rats who survived and can move and we will follow from a distance, but we must take care that we go unnoticed".

As they arrived at places of interest such as the woods where they had found Phoebe and where they had met the sheep, Sparky and Phoebe would tell of their adventures while Nelson led the way.

The stories helped to pass the time as they went, travelling without stopping to often only when they needed a drink from a puddel or a stream or to let Puddy rest for a while.

After a few days they arrived at the point where Fred had found them. Looking up at the hill it was decided that they would all rest for a while and then in the dark they would start the climb.

Sparky became very agitated and worried. "What if Granny Thelma is not on the other side of the hill, where will we look next and what about Puddy, she is realy poorly now" he thought.

His thoughts were interrupted by Nelson calling to them all that it was time to start the climb and so together they set off unaware, that not far behind, a group of rats were watching their every move.

Chapter 15...........Home!!

It was getting dark outside, so Granny Thelma went to the back door, turning on the outside light as she went. The light coming from the house spread into the garden and up to the fence lighting up the gate which was closed.

Every night since Sparky had vanished Granny Thelma had carried out the same ritual without fail. She would turn on the light, open the door and shout Sparky's name loudly for quite some time.

Then she would go back inside, sit in her chair, and cry herself to sleep. After a few hours she would wake up and go to the back door, look around again, and then go back inside closing the door behind her.

Sparky, Phoebe, Nelson and the Cat-gang were very tired. They had walked a lot today but had found no food so they were very hungry. Puddy's paw was getting worse and she was finding it hard to walk. They climbed the large hill, and when they got to the top they looked around them, but it was rather dark except for a glow coming from a small house below. "We are all tired and hungry" said Nelson" as he looked around but there came no reply from Sparky. Sparky was stood very still, with his mouth wide open and unable to say anything.

"What is the matter" Nelson shouted loudly in Sparky's ear.

After a short while Sparky looked at Nelson and said "There, past the woods, the little house with the light above the door, and the big tree in the garden"

"What about it" asked Nelson "its just a little house".

"Yes" replied Sparky "but its my house" he answered excitedly and he began running down the hill as fast as his little legs would go.

"Are you sure or have you just lost your mind "said Nelson out loudly but Sparky took no notice and continued running, so Nelson and the rest followed behind him.

Tigger and Fred walked either side of Puddy to support her as she went and they could only proceed at a slow pace.

Sparky began to bark as loudly and as happily as he could as he descended the hill.

Granny Thelma had been sitting in her chair for a short while when suddenly she thought she heard a dog barking.

"I must have been dreaming" she said to herself and was about to close her eyes when she heard the barking again.

"I'm not dreaming" she thought and got up from the chair and went to the back door as quickly as she could.

As she opened the door the light from inside spread itself across the garden and up to the fence and she switched on the outside light for extra brightness.

Now the sound of the barking was very loud, and she was sure it was
Sparky "it sounds so like him" she thought.

"Sparky, Sparky" she shouted as loudly as she could. "Where are you,
where are you".

Sparky stopped running and stood very still. "What's the matter "asked
Nelson, stopping beside Sparky and gasping for breath.

"I can hear Granny Thelma shouting my name" he replied and began
running toward the house again.

Granny Thelma ran as quickly as she could to the gate and opened it.

Sparky was near enough to see the gate open and this caused him to run
even faster.

Then in the dim light their eyes met and Sparky started to bark louder as
if he was afraid that Granny Thelma might not recognise him and at the
same time, Granny Thelma began to cry with excitement.

As if pre-arranged Granny Thelma held out her arms and Sparky gave a
tremendous leap.

Granny Thelma grabbed him in mid air and pulled him to her and
started to kiss his face and at the same time Sparky began to lick Granny
Thelma too.

"Where have you been" she asked him repeatedly as if expecting him to
reply but Sparky just licked her and whined with excitement.

Granny Thelma held Sparky tightly as if she believed he would disappear again if she let go.

Suddenly she heard a loud meow from near her feet.

She looked down to see another dog and some cats and then in the distance moving slowly came some more, one of which seemed to be hurt,

"O my goodness are they all with you"? she asked Sparky gently placing him onto the ground and walking over to where the slower group were approaching. She bent down and picked up Puddy.

"Where have you all come from?" she asked as looked them all over.

"You all look so hungry and this poor little thing has hurt her paw, come on in Sparky and bring your friends with you and I will find some food for you all and then see what I can do for this one" she said holding Puddy in her arms.

"If you have nowhere to go then you can all stay here, I am so glad to have Sparky back home and if you are his friends then you can all stay too".

"There, I told you that Granny Thelma would take care of us" he said to the group as they all followed Granny Thelma into the house.

Granny Thelma placed Puddy gently onto the floor and picked up Sparky again. "I can't believe you are back home again" she said to him as she held him tight.

Sparky licked her face and then she placed him back onto the floor.

"And look at this beautiful little doggy that you have with you and all of the pretty cats" she continued as she looked them all over.

Tigger watched everything that was happening with apprehension. He was used to being in charge and was not sure of what to make of all this fuss. Granny Thelma had even patted him and that was something that no one had done before.

Tigger looked around and felt quite at ease here. "Yes" he thought "This will be a lovely place to stay".

Granny Thelma went to the cupboard and removed some cans from it. "There we have some tuna for the cats" she said as she opened the cans and spread the contents onto a large tray.

She placed the tray down but before it even touched the floor the cats were eating from it except for Puddy. She was not feeling well and had no appetite.

Then she opened a can of dog food that she always had in her cupboard for Sparky and fed the two dogs.

"Right, I am going to take the little one, (not knowing Puddy's name she called her Little One) to the vet in the village. You are all to finish your food and then you are to make yourselves comfortable while I am away.

Tigger was not happy when he saw Granny Thelma putting Puddy into a

Basket, and the rest of the cat-gang were worried too, so they all started

to meow.

"I wont be long" she said and then she left the house.

Sensing that the cats were worried Sparky assured them that Granny

Thelma meant Puddy no harm, and so they all finished eating and then

began to explore the house.

They went into the living room where a fire was making the room lovely

and warm.

"You really do have a nice home" Nelson told Sparky and all of the

others agreed. They each found a comfortable place and settled down, but

Tigger was worried about Puddy, so he sat on the mat in front of the fire,

and watched the door.

Sparky jumped up onto the new settee and Phoebe jumped on too and

laid beside him.

Nelson, who had made himself comfortable on Granny Thelma's chair

looked at the two of them and smiled. "They look good together" he

thought and then, closing his eyes he went to sleep.

Fred, who was always alert found the silence a little nervy at first, but

being very tired, he too fell asleep on the carpet next to Tigger.

A noise woke them and they saw that Granny Thelma had returned with

Puddy.

Tigger was looking into the basket which was on the floor and was sniffing around, checking that Puddy was ok.

"I am fine" she told them and she showed them the bandage that was covering her paw.

Hearing that she was purring, the animals relaxed and began to settle back down.

Granny Thelma picked them all up in turn and gave then all a cuddle.

She was curious as to how Sparky had found so many friends and where they had all come from.

Did they have homes she asked herself, but then, remembering the way they looked and there condition, she assumed that they were all homeless and that Sparky had found them somewhere and had brought them home.

She did not mind of course, in fact ,she thought the extra company would be fun.

Picking up Nelson, she lifted the patch over his eye to see if he needed any sort of treatment but the area under the patch was clean so she placed the patch back over the eye and put him back down.

Tigger watched everything that Granny Thelma was doing and even though he was the leader, he felt no threat from her in fact he felt more comfortable here than he had ever felt before and hoped that they would all be able to stay.

Granny Thelma then made herself comfy in her chair so Nelson jumped up onto her lap.

Tigger took one more look around, and seeing that all was well, he returned to the mat in front of the fire and before long he and the rest of the animals were asleep.

Granny Thelma look around the living room. She saw that Sparky was watching her and she said "Well, you have brought home quite a family haven't you. I guess we are going to be one big happy family now". Sparky looked at her, and she was sure that she could see a smile on his face.

She made sure that Nelson was comfortable on her lap and then she closed her eyes and began to fall asleep.

Sparky had been silently watching Phoebe and the cats and Granny Thelma as they settled down. He jumped down from the settee and walked to the kitchen and seeing that the back door was still open, he looked outside.

The light was still on so he looked around the garden feeling safe and happy in his familiar surroundings.

He looked toward the gate and saw that it was shut.

"I will never go out there again "he thought to himself and turning around he started to walk back into the house.

Suddenly he stopped, looked back at the gate and smiled to himself.

"Well maybe never" he chuckled then walked into the living room.

Seeing that Granny Thelma and the animals were still asleep, he jumped

up onto the settee beside Phoebe and rubbed her nose with his. She

opened her eyes and smiled at him and then they cuddled in close to

each other.

Up on top of the hill two small heads appeared. Herk and Sneak looked

down at the little house.

"So that's where they are" Herk said to Sneak, "and they thought they

Had escaped from us".

"Good that they don't know, is it not" said Sneak.

"Good that they don't know what?" asked Herk.

"Good that they don't know that we know" replied Sneak.

"Good that they don't know that we know what?" asked Herk in an

annoyed voice.

"Good that they don't know what we know without them knowing it"

replied Sneak.

"WHAT are you talking about?" asked Herk in a now rather angry voice.

"Well" said Sneak, "I think that it is good that we know what we know

that they don't know because if they knew what we know then we would not be the only one's who know what we know but they would not know that we know what we know and we would know that we know that they know what we know without them knowing it" replied Sneak.

"I do not have the slightest idea as to what you are talking about" replied a now very angry Herk.

"Well it is really quite simple" answered Sneak, "if they knew what......

"Shut up" shouted Herk before Sneak could finish "not another word about what we know or do not know, I have had enough of your blabbering, not another sound do I want to hear from you until we get back to our hideout" Herk told Sneak sternly.

"But I..." Sneak began to say when a loud "NO" came from Herk, and looking once more at the little house and then back at Sneak, Herk turned and disappeared into the darkness.

"What is he so angry about?" thought Sneak to himself. If I can understand then why can't he understand that I understand what he does not understand when just because he does not understand then that does not mean to say that I don't understand what I am saying if....."
Suddenly Sneak stopped. "I think I need help" he said to himself worriedly and with that, he too turned and disappeared into the night.
Back at the house and having no idea that Herk and Sneak had found them, Sparky took one last look at all of his friends and Granny Thelma

and seeing that they were all sleeping, and so happy to be back home he moved closer to Phoebe and then, with thoughts of his adventure going through his mind, he too fell asleep.

The End ………………..???